A BANANA BOOK

STORM

Kevin Crossley-Holland

Illustrated by
ALAN MARKS

HEINEMANN·LONDON

For Kate, soon

First published in Great Britain 1985
by Heinemann Young Books
an imprint of Egmont Children's Books Limited
Michelin House, 81 Fulham Rd, London SW3 6RB

Reprinted in 1993, 1995, 1997 and 1998
Text copyright © 1985 Kevin Crossley-Holland
Illustrations copyright © 1985 Alan Marks

ISBN 0 434 903032 6

A CIP catalogue record for this book is available
at the British Library

Printed in Italy by Olivotto

A school pack of BANANA BOOKS 7-12 is available
from Heinemann Educational Books
ISBN 0 43500101 9

'SEVEN SWANS A-SWIMMING,' sang Annie, 'six geese a-laying . . .'

Annie was walking along the edge of the marsh, in no particular hurry because it was the first day of the Christmas holidays. After a while she began to practise clicking her fingers in time with the numbers. 'Three,' – CLICK! – 'three French hens, two,' – CLICK! – 'two turtle doves . . .'

Annie was used to being on her own. She was used to talking and singing to herself, and playing games like two-handed poohsticks and patience and solitaire. She really had no choice because her sister Willa was already grown up and married to Rod and expecting a baby and, anyhow, she lived fifty miles away.

Annie's parents, Mr and Mrs Carter, were rather old and not too well. Every day her mother complained that she felt as stiff as a whingeing hinge. 'It's that marsh,' she kept saying. 'The damp gets into my bones.' And since his stroke, her father was only able to walk with the help of two sticks. He had become quite mild and milky, like grain softened by mist.

Their cottage stood on its own at the edge of the great marsh, two miles away from the village of Waterslain. That marsh! Empty it looked and silent it seemed, but Annie knew better. She knew about the nests among the flags and rushes, she knew where to find the tunnels of the coypu and the dark pools teeming with shrimps and scooters. She knew the calls of the seabirds, the sucking sound of draining mud, the wind hissing in the sea lavender.

Every day in termtime Annie had to walk along this track at the edge of the marsh. She had to take off her shoes and socks to paddle across the ford of the river Rush, the little stream that bumbled all summer but burbled and bustled all winter when it was sometimes as much as twenty paces across. And then she hurried up the pot-holed lane to the crossroads where the school bus picked her up at twenty-to-nine and took her into Waterslain.

The only thing that Annie didn't like were the steely winter days when it began to grow dark before she came home from school. The marsh didn't seem such a friendly place then. The wind whined, seabirds screamed. At night, the boggarts and bogles and other marsh spirits showed their horrible faces. Once, Annie had heard the Shuck, the monster dog, coming up behind her and had only just got indoors in time.

Worst of all was the ghost who haunted the ford. Annie's mother said that he didn't mean to harm anyone, he just liked to play tricks on them and scare them. On one occasion Mrs Carter had dropped a basket of shopping into the water, and she complained the ghost had given her a push from behind. And the farmer,

Mr Elkins, told Annie he had heard shouting and whinnying at the ford, but could see no man or horse to go with them. Annie always ran down the lane after school in winter so that she could get past the ford before it was completely dark.

'Two turtle doves,' sang Annie – CLICK! – 'and a partridge in a pear tree.'

'An-nie! An-nie!'

Annie turned round and saw her mother standing at the door of their cottage, waving.

'What?' she shouted. 'What is it?' But the wind picked up her words and carried them off in the wrong direction. And why, wondered Annie, why have I got to go in when I was just going out?

'Lunch!' called her mother as soon as she heard Annie open the door and felt a tide of chill air washing round her ankles.

'Your sister's just been on the telephone. She's coming home tomorrow.'

'Willa!' cried Annie.

'You know the baby's due on Christmas Day?'

'Of course I know,' said Annie.

'Well, Willa says Rod can't get home now until early in the New Year.'

'Why not?' asked Annie.

'Just when she needs him,' said Annie's mother. 'Can you imagine? Thousands of miles away on the Indian Ocean.'

'I wouldn't like to marry a sailor,' said Annie.

'So she's coming home tomorrow,' her mother repeated, and then she smiled at Annie. 'She wants a bit of company.'

'What about the baby?' asked Annie.

'She'll have the baby in the cottage hospital,' said her mother. 'Doctor

Grant has arranged that.'

'How long will she be in there?'

'Two days or seven days,' said Annie's mother. 'That's the rule.'

'Two, I hope,' said Annie. 'Then it can sleep in my room.'

'It can sleep with Willa,' said her mother. 'Oh! That marsh. The damp gets into my bones.'

The next day, Annie and her mother crossed the ford and walked up to the crossroads and met Willa off the afternoon bus.

'What a journey!' said Willa.

'Two changes?' asked her mother.

'Three!' said Willa. 'This place is miles from anywhere.'

Annie said nothing. She had never thought of her home and the great marsh as miles from anywhere. To her, they were everywhere, everywhere that really mattered.

'Miles!' said Willa again. 'Hello, Annie!'

Annie felt quite shy as she kissed her sister. Perhaps Willa felt shy too. It always took them a few minutes before they got used to each other and found it easy to talk to each other again.

But once Annie and Willa began to talk, there was no stopping them.

They talked at breakfast and lunch and tea. They talked in between times. They talked as they walked along the marsh track and talked their way along the legs of the dyke that led out to the booming sea.

Willa told Annie what it felt like to be having a baby and Annie told Willa about school in Waterslain – the same

school Willa had attended when she was a girl. Willa told Annie about town life. Annie told Willa the names of plants and birds.

'I never did learn them,' said Willa, 'and I always wish I had.'

When they came to the ford, Annie asked Willa about the ghost.

'He's here, all right. He's here,' said Willa. 'You know the story.'

'What story?' asked Annie.

'When he was alive – I mean when he had a body – he used to own Mr Elkins' farm. That was in the days when there were highwaymen. Two of them ambushed him right here.'

Annie felt a cold finger slowly moving from the base of her spine up to her neck, and then spreading out across her shoulders.

'Where we're standing,' said Willa.

'What happened?' asked Annie.

'He wouldn't give them his money,' said Willa. 'He was that brave. So they killed him and his horse.'

'His horse!' cried Annie. 'That's horrible!' And at once she began to think of her lonely walks back from school – the dark January journeys lying in wait for her.

'So they got his money anyhow,' said Willa. 'That's what I've heard.'

'And the ghost?' said Annie.

'That goes up and down and around and pays out passers by,' said Willa. The sisters fell silent and stared at the flashing water.

On the third night after Willa came home there was a tremendous storm. Annie lay warm in her bed and listened to the wind going wild outside. It bumped and blundered against the walls of the cottage, it whistled between its salty lips and gnashed its sharp teeth.

As Annie dozed, she began to imagine she was not in bed but in a boat, rocking, quite safe, far out at sea. The sheets of rain lashing at her little window were small waves smacking at the bows, streaming down the boat's sides . . .

This was the night on which Willa's baby decided to be born. Just before midnight, it began to heave inside its mother like a buoy on surging water.

Everyone got up. Willa and Annie and their mother and even their father. All the lights were turned on again. The kettle began to sing.

'A cup of tea first,' said Annie's mother, looking pleased and shiny.

'You said Christmas,' protested Annie.

'You never can tell,' said her mother. 'Anyhow, early or late, storm or no storm, it's on its way. There's no stopping it now!'

'You could call it Storm,' said Mr Carter unexpectedly.

'That's not a name,' said Annie.

'Storm?' said Willa.

'Storm,' repeated Annie's mother. 'That's an old name in these parts.'

'Shall I ring the hospital?' said Willa. 'I know there's time but . . .'

'I'll ring while you get yourself

packed and ready,' said her mother.

'Ask them to come for me in half-an-hour,' said Willa and, taking her tea with her, she went back upstairs to get ready.

When Annie's mother lifted the receiver, she first looked worried, and then she looked really alarmed.

'What's wrong?' said Mr Carter.

'Come and listen to this,' said Annie's mother.

Mr Carter dragged himself across the room and put an ear to the black receiver. Then he banged the telephone with the palm of his hand. He listened again. There was not a sound.

'Blast!' said Mr Carter. 'The lines are down.'

'What,' said Annie's mother, 'are we going to do?'

If anything, the storm was even fiercer now than it had been before. There was a howl of wind and a grating noise overhead, then outside the window a smash.

'Blast!' said Mr Carter. 'That's a tile gone.'

'What are we going to do, Bill?' repeated Annie's mother. 'We must get Doctor Grant. You can't walk and I must stay in case . . .'

'I'll go,' said Annie.

'No, no,' said her mother.

'I'm the only one who can,' Annie said. She had the strange feeling that it wasn't her but someone else speaking.

Mrs Carter frowned and shook her head.

'We can't do without a doctor,' said Annie. 'Willa can't.'

Annie's mother looked worried. 'It's the only way, Annie,' she said. 'We'll get you well wrapped up and you'll be all right. Go straight to Doctor Grant. Ask him to ring the hospital for an ambulance and then come at once himself.'

For once Annie took care over getting ready to go out. While her mother fussed round her and Willa sat very calm and upright on her bed, she put on her underclothes and then her track suit and then an old mackintosh over that. Her mother stuffed a handtowel into one pocket and slipped a bar of chocolate into the other.

'I'll need my sou' wester,' said Annie. She picked up the hat from the floor, jammed it on and tied the lace under her chin.

'And your Wellingtons,' said her mother.

'What else?' said Annie. 'My scarf.'

'A torch,' said her mother. 'Though you know the way so well by now you could walk there backwards.'

'You're a real sport, Annie,' said Willa.

'It's only the ford I don't like,' said Annie. 'I don't mind the rest.'

'I know,' said Annie's mother. 'Make sure you dry yourself properly.'

'You'll soon get past it,' said Willa. Then she gasped, pressed the palms of her hands against her stomach, and breathed deeply. 'This baby,' she said. 'I think it's in a hurry.'

When Mrs Carter opened the cottage door, the wind snatched it out of her hands and slammed the door against the wall.

'Blast!' said Mr Carter. 'That's a rough old night!'

The four of them stood just inside the door, huddled together, staring out, getting used to the storm and the darkness.

There was a slice of moon well up

in the sky. It seemed to be speeding behind grey lumpy clouds, running away from something that was chasing it. The Carters' little garden looked ashen and the marsh looked ashen and Mr Elkins' fields looked ashen.

They all heard it then: the sound of hooves, galloping.

'Blast!' said Mr Carter. 'Who can that be, then?'

'In this storm!' cried Annie's mother.

'At midnight,' said Mr Carter.

Annie slipped one hand inside her mother's hand. The hooves drummed louder and louder, almost on top of them, and round the corner of the cottage galloped a horseman on a fine chestnut mare.

'Whoa!' shouted the rider when he saw Annie and her family standing at the cottage door.

'That's not Elkins, then,' said Mr Carter, hauling himself in front of his wife and daughters. 'That's not his horse.'

The horseman stopped just outside the pool of light streaming through the open door, and none of them recognised him. He was tall and unsmiling.

'That's a rough old night,' Mr Carter called out.

The horseman nodded and said not a word.

'Are you going into Waterslain?'

'Waterslain?' said the horseman. 'Not in particular.'

'Blast!' said Mr Carter in a thoughtful kind of way.

'I could go,' said the horseman in a dark voice, 'if there was a need.'

Then Annie's mother loosed her daughter's hand and stepped out into the storm and soon explained the need, and Mr Carter went out and asked the horseman his name. The wind gave a shriek and Annie was unable to catch his reply. 'So you see,' said Annie's mother, 'there's no time to be lost.'

'Come on up, Annie,' said the horseman.

'It's all right,' said Annie, shaking her head.

'I'll take you,' said the horseman.

'You'll be fine,' said Mrs Carter.

'I can walk,' insisted Annie.

But the horseman quickly bent down and put a hand under one of Annie's shoulders and swung her up onto the saddle in front of him as if she were as light as thistledown.

Annie's heart was beating fearfully.
She bit hard on her lower lip.

Then the horseman raised one hand
and spurred his horse. Mr and Mrs
Carter stood and watched as Annie
turned away the full white moon of
her face and then she and the
horseman were swallowed in the
stormy darkness.

At first Annie said nothing and the
horseman said nothing. But as the
horse slowed to a trot and then began
to wade across the ford, the horseman
asked quietly, 'Are you afraid, Annie?'

'I am,' said Annie. 'I'm afraid for
my sister and her baby,' she said.
'And I'm afraid of meeting the ghost.'
She paused and then added in a sort of
sob, 'I think I'd die if I met him
tonight.'

At first the horseman didn't reply,
and Annie thought it best not to say
anything about being rather afraid of
him as well, not knowing who he was.

But then the rider suddenly reined in. 'Annie,' he said, 'your sister and her baby will be all right.'

'How do you know?' asked Annie.

'And you'll be all right,' said the horseman. 'There are ghosts and ghosts, Annie. Kind ghosts and unkind ghosts. You won't meet the ghost you fear between here and Waterslain.'

And so, step by step, Annie and the horseman slowly crossed the ford.

Now the chestnut mare quickened her stride again. It comforted Annie to feel the mare's warm neck and flanks, and after a while she leaned forward and buried her face in its mane.

With her eyes closed, Annie had the sense that she was not so much riding as flying – flying through the storm on a journey that might last forever.

He's a ghost himself, thought Annie. He's bewitched us all and he's taking me away. He's taking me away into the always-darkness. No! No! That's wrong. No, he's my helper and we're going to the rescue of a maiden in distress.

When she sat up again, Annie felt quite dizzy. She shook her head and frowned. 'That's silly,' she told herself. 'You've been reading too many tales.'

And yet, wondered Annie, who is this rider? Where does he come from? And how did he happen to gallop right past our door just when we needed him? 'What's your name?' called Annie over her shoulder.

'What's that?' said the horseman. 'My name? Storm!'

'Storm!' cried Annie. 'That's even stranger.'

What a night it was! The salty wind was going round and round in circles, first whipping them forward, then holding them up, then barging them towards the hedge on one side of the lane or the deep ditch on the other.

The horseman kept one arm round Annie and Annie held onto the horse. The rain flew straight at them, spiteful drops sharp as pins and needles.

Then Annie began to sway in the saddle. She thought she could bear it no longer – the furious gallop, the gallop of the storm, the storm of her own fears. What can I do, she thought. What can I do? What if I never get to Doctor Grant?

But the horseman only shouted and spurred his horse to go even faster. He seemed bent on going where he was going as quickly as he possibly could. Faster and faster! So that when Annie looked about her again, there she was! There she was in sleeping Waterslain. The chestnut mare was sweating and blowing out big puffs of condensed air.

'Down Staithe Street,' gasped
Annie. 'Doctor Grant.'

The horseman galloped straight up
the middle of the village street. The
horse's hooves clattered on the tarmac
and Annie saw that several times they
struck sparks from pieces of chert and
flint. Then they turned into Staithe
Street and 'Whoa!' shouted the
horseman in his dark voice.

'Whoa!' And his mare at last slowed
down to a trot.

'There!' said Annie, pointing to a
gateway flanked by laurel bushes.
'We're there!'

Doctor Grant's lights were still on.
His curtains were the colour of ripe
peaches. And a lantern, swaying in his
porch, threw a pool of soft shifting
light over the flagstones and gravel
outside the front door.

Annie stared and stared as if she had never seen bright light before. In the gloom of the great storm, nothing had looked quite definite and many things looked frightening: the reaching arms of the tree, the fallen body of the milk churn, the gleam and flash of water. There was the danger, too, of meeting these chancy things that only come out at night – will-o'-the-wykes and bogles and boggarts and the black dog, Shuck . . . and worst of all there was the ghost. But now, in the clear light, there was no longer room for anything uncertain or ghostly.

Annie relaxed her grip on the horse and took a deep breath. And when she slowly let her breath out again, she felt as if she had been holding it in ever since she left home.

'So, Annie,' said the horseman, 'this is where I must leave you.'

'Come in!' cried Annie. 'I'm sure
you can come in.'

'You must go your way and I mine,'

said the horseman, shaking his head, and taking great care to stop his horse from putting so much as a hoof into the pool of light. 'Your sister and her baby will be all right.'

So Annie swung down out of the saddle and stood on the gravel, feeling rather shaky. She looked up at the man, still unsmiling and sitting so still.

'Thank you,' cried Annie. 'Thank you. I was so afraid.' She shook her head. 'I was afraid of meeting the ghost.'

'There was no fear of that,' said the horseman. 'Annie,' he said, 'I *am* the ghost.'

Annie drew in her breath with a sob. She raised her arms and for one second closed her eyes as tight as cockleshells.

When she opened them again there was nobody there, no horseman and no horse.

Dr Grant's lantern still creaked and swayed in the porch, and its light shone over the flagstones and gravel, but Storm and his chestnut mare, they had both completely vanished.